VIRGINIA WOOLF

Virginia Woolf was born in 1882, the youngest daughter of writer Sir Leslie Stephen. She was educated at home with her sister, Vanessa. The death of Woolf's mother in 1895 and her father in 1904 led to the first of the serious nervous breakdowns that would feature heavily in her life. Shortly afterwards, she moved with her siblings to 46 Gordon Square, the first meeting place of the Bloomsbury Group, a literary and artistic circle. In 1912, Virginia finished a draft of her first novel, *The Voyage Out*, and married Leonard Woolf. They would subsequently found the Hogarth Press. Eight more novels followed, including *Mrs Dalloway* (1925) and *To the Lighthouse* (1927), establishing her position as one of the twentieth century's most important modernist writers. Woolf died by suicide in 1941.

VIRGINIA WOOLF

An Unwritten Novel

M
10

'A Haunted House' first published 1921
'Kew Gardens' first published 1919
'Solid Objects' and 'An Unwritten Novel' first published 1920
'The New Dress' first published 1927
'The Lady in the Looking-Glass' first published 1929
'The Mark on the Wall' first published 1917

This edition first published 2026 by Macmillan Collector's Library
an imprint of Pan Macmillan
The Smithson, 6 Briset Street, London EC1M 5NR
EU representative: Macmillan Publishers Ireland Ltd, 1st Floor,
The Liffey Trust Centre, 117–126 Sheriff Street Upper,
Dublin 1 D01 YC43
Associated companies throughout the world

ISBN 978-1-0374-0348-4

1 3 5 7 9 8 6 4 2

A CIP catalogue record for this book is available from the British Library.

Cover design: Tiana-Jane Dunlop, Pan Macmillan Art Department
Typeset in Adobe Caslon Pro by Six Red Marbles UK, Thetford, Norfolk
Printed and bound in the UK using 100% Renewable Electricity by CPI Group (UK) Ltd

CONTENTS

A Haunted House

Whatever hour you woke there was a door shutting. From room to room they went, hand in hand, lifting here, opening there, making sure—a ghostly couple.

"Here we left it," she said. And he added, "Oh, but here too!" "It's upstairs," she murmured, "And in the garden," he whispered. "Quietly," they said, "or we shall wake them."

But it wasn't that you woke us. Oh, no. "They're looking for it; they're drawing the curtain" one might say, and so read on a page or two. "Now they've found it," one would be certain, stopping the pencil on the margin. And then, tired of reading, one might rise and see for oneself, the house all empty, the doors standing open, only the wood pigeons bubbling with content and the hum of the threshing machine sounding from the farm. "What did I come in here for? What did I want to find?" My hands were empty. "Perhaps it's upstairs then?" The apples were in the loft. And so down again, the garden still as ever, only the book had slipped into the grass.

But they had found it in the drawing room. Not that one could ever see them. The window panes reflected apples, reflected roses; all the leaves were green in the glass. If they moved in the drawing room, the apple only turned its yellow side. Yet, the moment after, if the door was opened, spread about the floor, hung upon the walls, pendant from the ceiling—what? My hands were empty. The shadow of a thrush crossed the carpet; from the deepest wells of silence the wood pigeon drew its bubble of sound. "Safe, safe, safe," the pulse of the house beat softly. "The treasure buried; the room . . ." the pulse stopped short. Oh, was that the buried treasure?

A moment later the light had faded. Out in the garden then? But the trees spun darkness for a wandering beam of sun. So fine, so rare, coolly sunk beneath the surface the beam I sought always burnt behind the glass. Death was the glass; death was between us; coming to the woman first, hundreds of years ago, leaving the house, sealing all the windows; the rooms were darkened. He left it, left her, went North, went East, saw the stars turned in the Southern sky; sought the house, found it dropped beneath the Downs. "Safe, safe, safe," the pulse of the house beat gladly, "The treasure yours."

The wind roars up the avenue. Trees stoop and bend this way and that. Moonbeams splash and spill wildly in the rain. But the beam of the lamp falls straight from the window. The candle burns stiff and still. Wandering through the house, opening the windows, whispering not to wake us, the ghostly couple seek their joy.

"Here we slept," she says. And he adds, "Kisses without number." "Waking in the morning—" "Silver between the trees—" "Upstairs—" "In the garden—" "When summer came—" "In winter snowtime—" The doors go shutting far in the distance, gently knocking like the pulse of a heart.

Nearer they come; cease at the doorway. The wind falls, the rain slides silver down the glass. Our eyes darken; we hear no steps beside us; we see no lady spread her ghostly cloak. His hands shield the lantern. "Look," he breathes. "Sound asleep. Love upon their lips."

Stooping, holding their silver lamp above us, long they look and deeply. Long they pause. The wind drives straightly; the flame stoops slightly. Wild beams of moonlight cross both floor and wall, and, meeting, stain the faces bent; the faces pondering; the faces that search the sleepers and seek their hidden joy.

"Safe, safe, safe," the heart of the house beats proudly. "Long years—" he sighs. "Again you found me." "Here," she murmurs, "sleeping; in the garden reading; laughing, rolling apples in the loft. Here we left our treasure—" Stooping, their light lifts the lids upon my eyes. "Safe! safe! safe!" the pulse of the house beats wildly. Waking, I cry "Oh, is *this* your buried treasure? The light in the heart."

Kew Gardens

From the oval shaped flower-bed there rose perhaps a hundred stalks spreading into heart shaped or tongue shaped leaves half way up and unfurling at the tip red or blue or yellow petals marked with spots of colour raised upon the surface; and from the red, blue or yellow gloom of the throat emerged a straight bar, rough with gold dust and slightly clubbed at the end. The petals were voluminous enough to be stirred by the summer breeze, and when they moved, the red blue and yellow lights passed one over the other, staining an inch of the brown earth beneath with a spot of the most intricate colour. The light fell either upon the smooth grey back of a pebble, or the shell of a snail with its brown circular veins, or, falling into a raindrop, it expanded with such intensity of red, blue and yellow the thin walls of water that one expected them to burst and disappear. Instead, the drop was left in a second silver grey once more, and the light now settled upon the flesh of a leaf, revealing the branching thread of fibre beneath the surface, and again it moved on and spread its illumination in the vast green spaces beneath the dome of the heart shaped and tongue shaped leaves. Then the breeze stirred rather more briskly overhead and the colour was flashed into the air above, into the eyes of the men and women who walk in Kew Gardens in July.

The figures of these men and women straggled past the flower-bed with a curiously irregular movement not unlike that of the white and blue butterflies who crossed the turf in zig-zag flights from bed to bed. The man was about six inches in front of the woman, strolling carelessly, while she bore on with greater purpose, only turning her head now and then to see that the children were not too far behind. The man kept this distance in front of the woman purposely, though perhaps unconsciously, for he wished to go on with his thoughts.

"Fifteen years ago I came here with Lily," he thought. "We sat somewhere over there by a lake, and I begged her to marry me all through the hot afternoon. How the dragonfly kept circling round us: how clearly I see the dragonfly and her shoe with the square silver buckle at the toe. All the time I spoke I saw her shoe and when it moved impatiently I knew without looking up what she was going to say: the whole of her seemed to be in her shoe. And my love, my desire, were in the dragonfly; for some reason I thought that if it settled there, on that leaf, the broad one with the red flower in the middle of it, if the dragonfly settled on the leaf she would say "Yes" at once. But the dragonfly went round and round: it never settled anywhere—of course not, happily not, or I shouldn't be walking here with Eleanor and the children—Tell me, Eleanor. D'you ever think of the past?"

"Why do you ask, Simon?"

"Because I've been thinking of the past. I've been

thinking of Lily, the woman I might have married . . . Well, why are you silent? Do you mind my thinking of the past?"

"Why should I mind, Simon? Doesn't one always think of the past, in a garden with men and women lying under the trees? Aren't they one's past, all that remains of it, those men and women, those ghosts lying under the trees, . . . one's happiness, one's reality?"

"For me, a square silver shoe buckle and a dragonfly—"

"For me, a kiss. Imagine six little girls sitting before their easels twenty years ago, down by the side of a lake, painting the water-lilies, the first red water-lilies I'd ever seen. And suddenly a kiss, there on the back of my neck. And, my hand shook all the afternoon so that I couldn't paint. I took out my watch and marked the hour when I would allow myself to think of the kiss for five minutes only—it was so precious—the kiss of an old grey-haired woman with a wart on her nose, the mother of all my kisses all my life. Come Caroline, come Hubert."

They walked on past the flower-bed, now walking four abreast, and soon diminished in size among the trees and looked half transparent as the sunlight and shade swam over their backs in large trembling irregular patches.

In the oval flower bed the snail, whose shell had been stained red, blue, and yellow for the space of two minutes or so, now appeared to be moving very slightly in its shell, and next began to labour over the crumbs of loose earth which broke away and rolled down as it passed over them. It appeared to have a definite goal in front of it, differing in this respect from the singular high stepping angular green insect who attempted to cross in front of it, and waited for a second with its antennae trembling as if in deliberation, and then stepped off as rapidly and strangely in the opposite direction. Brown cliffs with deep green lakes in the hollows, flat blade-like trees that waved from root to tip, round boulders of grey stone, vast crumpled surfaces of a thin crackling texture—all these objects lay across the snail's progress between one stalk and another to his goal. Before he had decided whether to circumvent the arched tent of a dead leaf or to breast it there came past the bed the feet of other human beings.

This time they were both men. The younger of the two wore an expression of perhaps unnatural calm; he raised his eyes and fixed them very steadily in front of him while his companion spoke, and directly his companion had done speaking he looked on the ground again and sometimes opened his lips only after a long pause and sometimes did not open them at all. The elder man had a curiously uneven and shaky method of walking, jerking his hand forward and throwing up his head abruptly, rather in the manner of an impatient carriage horse tired of waiting outside a house; but in the man these gestures were irresolute and pointless. He talked almost incessantly; he smiled to himself and again began to talk, as if the smile had been an answer. He was talking about spirits—the spirits of the dead, who, according to him, were even now telling him all sorts of odd things about their experiences in Heaven.

"Heaven was known to the ancients as Thessaly, William, and now, with this war, the spirit matter is rolling between the hills like thunder." He paused, seemed to listen, smiled, jerked his head and continued:—

"You have a small electric battery and a piece of rubber to insulate the wire—isolate?—insulate?—well, we'll skip the details, no good going into details that wouldn't be understood—and in short the little machine stands in any convenient position by the head of the bed, we will say, on a neat mahogany stand. All arrangements being properly fixed by workmen under my direction, the widow applies her ear and summons the spirit by sign as agreed. Women! Widows! Women in black——"

Here he seemed to have caught sight of a woman's dress in the distance, which in the shade looked a purple black. He took off his hat, placed his hand upon his heart, and hurried towards her muttering and gesticulating feverishly. But William caught him by the sleeve and touched a flower with the tip of his walking-stick in order to divert the old man's attention. After looking at it for a moment in some confusion the old man bent his ear to it and seemed to answer a voice speaking from it, for he began talking about the forests of Uruguay which he had visited hundreds of years ago in company with the most beautiful young woman in Europe. He could be heard murmuring about forests of Uruguay blanketed with the wax petals of tropical roses, nightingales, sea beaches, mermaids, and women drowned at sea, as he suffered himself to be moved on by William, upon whose face the look of stoical patience grew slowly deeper and deeper.

Following his steps so closely as to be slightly puzzled

by his gestures came two elderly women of the lower middle class, one stout and ponderous, the other rosy cheeked and nimble. Like most people of their station they were frankly fascinated by any signs of eccentricity betokening a disordered brain, especially in the well-to-do; but they were too far off to be certain whether the gestures were merely eccentric or genuinely mad. After they had scrutinised the old man's back in silence for a moment and given each other a queer, sly look, they went on energetically piecing together their very complicated dialogue:

"Nell, Bert, Lot, Cess, Phil, Pa, he says, I says, she says, I says, I says, I says——"

"My Bert, Sis, Bill, Grandad, the old man, sugar,
Sugar, flour, kippers, greens,
Sugar, sugar, sugar."

The ponderous woman looked through the pattern of falling words at the flowers standing cool, firm, and upright in the earth, with a curious expression. She saw them as a sleeper waking from a heavy sleep sees a brass candlestick reflecting the light in an unfamiliar way, and closes his eyes and opens them, and seeing the brass candlestick again, finally starts broad awake and stares at the candlestick with all his powers. So the heavy woman came to a standstill opposite the oval shaped flower bed, and ceased even to pretend to listen to what the other woman was saying. She stood there letting the words fall over her, swaying the top part of her body slowly backwards and forwards, looking at the flowers. Then she suggested that they should find a seat and have their tea.

The snail had now considered every possible method

of reaching his goal without going round the dead leaf or climbing over it. Let alone the effort needed for climbing a leaf, he was doubtful whether the thin texture which vibrated with such an alarming crackle when touched even by the tip of his horns would bear his weight; and this determined him finally to creep beneath it, for there was a point where the leaf curved high enough from the ground to admit him. He had just inserted his head in the opening and was taking stock of the high brown roof and was getting used to the cool brown light when two other people came past outside on the turf. This time they were both young, a young man and a young woman. They were both in the prime of youth, or even in that season which precedes the prime of youth, the season before the smooth pink folds of the flower have burst their gummy case, when the wings of the butterfly, though fully grown, are motionless in the sun.

"Lucky it isn't Friday," he observed.

"Why? D'you believe in luck?"

"They make you pay sixpence on Friday."

"What's sixpence anyway? Isn't it worth sixpence?"

"What's 'it'—what do you mean by 'it'?"

"O anything—I mean—you know what I mean."

Long pauses came between each of these remarks; they were uttered in toneless and monotonous voices. The couple stood still on the edge of the flower-bed, and together pressed the end of her parasol deep down into the soft earth. The action and the fact that his hand rested on the top of hers expressed their feelings in a strange way, as these short insignificant words also expressed something, words with short wings for their heavy body of meaning, inadequate to carry them far and thus alighting awkwardly upon the very common objects that surrounded them, and were to their inexperienced touch so massive; but who knows (so they thought as they pressed the parasol into the earth) what precipices aren't concealed in them, or what slopes of ice don't shine in the sun on the other side? Who knows? Who has ever seen this before? Even when she wondered what sort of tea they gave you at Kew, he felt that something loomed up behind her words, and stood vast and solid behind them; and the mist very slowly rose and uncovered—O Heavens, what were those shapes?—little white tables, and waitresses who looked first at her and then at him; and there was a bill that he would pay with a real two shilling piece, and it was real, all real, he assured himself, fingering the coin in his pocket, real to everyone except to him and to her; even to him it began to seem real; and then—but it was too exciting to stand and think any longer, and he pulled the parasol out of the earth with a jerk and was impatient to find the place where one had tea with other people, like other people.

"Come along, Trissie; it's time we had our tea."

"Wherever *does* one have one's tea?" she asked with the oddest thrill of excitement in her voice, looking vaguely round and letting herself be drawn on down the grass path, trailing her parasol, turning her head this way and that way, forgetting her tea, wishing to go down there and then down there, remembering orchids and cranes among wild flowers, a Chinese pagoda and a crimson crested bird; but he bore her on.

Thus one couple after another with much the same irregular and aimless movement passed the flower-bed and were enveloped in layer after layer of green blue vapour, in which at first their bodies had substance and a dash of colour, but later both substance and colour dissolved in the green-blue atmosphere. How hot it was! So hot that even the thrush chose to hop, like a mechanical bird, in the shadow of the flowers, with long pauses between one movement and the next; instead of rambling vaguely the white butterflies danced one above another, making with their white shifting flakes the outline of a shattered marble column above the tallest flowers; the glass roofs of the palm house shone as if a whole market full of shiny green umbrellas had opened in the sun; and in the drone of the aeroplane the voice of the summer sky murmured its fierce soul. Yellow and black, pink and snow white, shapes of all these colours, men, women, and children were spotted for a second upon the horizon, and then, seeing the breadth of yellow that lay upon the grass, they wavered and sought shade beneath the trees, dissolving like drops of water in the yellow and green atmosphere, staining it faintly with red and blue. It seemed as if all gross and heavy bodies had sunk down in the heat motionless and lay huddled upon the ground, but their voices went wavering from them as if they were flames lolling from the thick waxen bodies of candles. Voices. Yes, voices. Wordless voices, breaking the silence suddenly with such depth of contentment, such passion of desire, or, in the voices of children, such freshness of surprise; breaking the silence? But there was no silence; all the time the motor omnibuses were turning their wheels and changing their gear; like a vast nest of Chinese boxes all of wrought steel turning ceaselessly one within another the city murmured; on the top of which the voices cried aloud and the petals of myriads of flowers flashed their colours into the air.

Solid Objects

The only thing that moved upon the vast semicircle of the beach was one small black spot. As it came nearer to the ribs and spine of the stranded pilchard boat, it became apparent from a certain tenuity in its blackness that this spot possessed four legs: and moment by moment it became more unmistakable that it was composed of the persons of two young men. Even thus in outline against the sand there was an unmistakable vitality in them; an indescribable vigour in the approach and withdrawal of the bodies, slight though it was, which proclaimed some violent argument issuing from the tiny mouths of the little round heads. This was corroborated on closer view by the repeated lunging of a walking-stick on the right-hand side. "You mean to tell me . . . You actually believe . . ." thus the walking-stick on the right-hand side next the waves seemed to be asserting as it cut long straight stripes upon the sand.

"Politics be damned!" issued clearly from the body on the left-hand side, and, as these words were uttered, the mouths, noses, chins, little moustaches, tweed caps, rough boots, shooting coats, and check stockings of the two speakers became clearer and clearer; the smoke of their pipes went up into the air; nothing was so solid, so living, so hard, red, hirsute and virile as these two bodies for miles and miles of sea and sandhill.

They flung themselves down by the six ribs and spine of the black pilchard boat. You know how the body seems to shake itself free from an argument, and to apologize for a mood of exaltation; flinging itself down and expressing in the looseness of its attitude a readiness to take up with something new—whatever it may be that comes next to hand. So Charles, whose stick had been slashing the beach for half a mile or so, began skimming flat pieces of slate over the water; and John, who had exclaimed " Politics be damned!" began burrowing his fingers down, down, into the sand. As his hand went further and further beyond the wrist, so that he had to hitch his sleeve a little higher, his eyes lost their intensity, or rather the background of thought and experience which gives an inscrutable depth to the eyes of grown people disappeared, leaving only the clear transparent surface, expressing nothing but wonder, which the eyes of young children display. No doubt the act of burrowing in the sand had something to do with it. He remembered that, after digging for a little, the water oozes round your finger-tips; the hole then becomes a moat; a well; a spring; a secret channel to the sea. As he was choosing which of these things to make it, still working his fingers in the water, they curled round something hard—a full drop of solid matter—and gradually dislodged a large irregular lump, and brought it to the surface. When the sand coating was wiped off, a green tint appeared. It was a lump of glass, so thick as to be almost opaque; the smoothing of the sea had completely worn off any edge or shape, so that it was impossible to say whether it had been bottle, tumbler or window-pane; it was nothing but glass; it was almost a precious stone. You had only to enclose it in a rim of gold, or pierce it with a wire, and it became a jewel; part of a necklace, or a dull, green light upon a finger. Perhaps after all it was really a gem; something worn by a dark Princess trailing her finger in the water as she sat in the stern of the boat and listened to the slaves singing as they rowed her across the Bay. Or the oak sides of a sunk Elizabethan treasure-chest had split apart, and, rolled over and over, over and over, its emeralds had come at last to shore. John turned it in his hands; he held it to the light; he held it so that its irregular mass blotted out the body and extended right arm of his friend. The green thinned and thickened slightly as it was held against the sky or against the body. It pleased him; it puzzled him; it was so hard, so concentrated, so definite an object compared with the vague sea and the hazy shore.

Now a sigh disturbed him—profound, final, making him aware that his friend Charles had thrown all the flat stones within reach, or had come to the conclusion that it was not worth while to throw them. They ate their sandwiches side by side. When they had done, and were shaking themselves and rising to their feet, John took the lump of glass and looked at it in silence. Charles looked at it too. But he saw immediately that it was not flat, and filling his pipe he said with the energy that dismisses a foolish strain of thought,

"To return to what I was saying——"

He did not see, or if he had seen would hardly have noticed, that John after looking at the lump for a moment, as if in hesitation, slipped it inside his pocket. That impulse, too may have been the impulse which leads a child to pick up one pebble on a path strewn with them, promising it a life of warmth and security upon the nursery mantelpiece, delighting in the sense of power and benignity which such an action confers, and believing that the heart of the stone leaps with joy when it sees itself chosen from a million like it, to enjoy this bliss instead of a life of cold and wet upon the high road. "It might so easily have been any other of the millions of stones, but it was I, I, I!"

Whether this thought or not was in John's mind; the lump of glass had its place upon the mantelpiece, where it stood heavy upon a little pile of bills and letters, and served not only as an excellent paper-weight, but also as a natural stopping place for the young man's eyes when they wandered from his book. Looked at again and again half consciously by a mind thinking of something else, any object mixes itself so profoundly with the stuff of thought that it loses its actual form and recomposes itself a little differently in an ideal shape which haunts the brain when we least expect it. So John found himself attracted to the windows of curiosity shops when he was out walking, merely because he saw something which reminded him of the lump of glass. Anything, so long as it was an object of some kind, more or less round, perhaps with a dying flame deep sunk in its mass, anything—china, glass, amber, rock, marble—even the smooth oval egg of a prehistoric bird would do. He took, also, to keeping his eyes upon the ground, especially in the neighbourhood of waste land where the household refuse is thrown away. Such objects often occurred there—thrown away, of no use to anybody, shapeless, discarded. In a few months he had collected four or five specimens that took their place upon the mantelpiece. They were useful, too, for a man who is standing for Parliament upon the brink of a brilliant career has any number of papers to keep in order—addresses to constituents, declarations of policy, appeals for subscriptions, invitations to dinner, and so on.

One day, starting from his rooms in the Temple to catch a train in order to address his constituents, his eyes rested upon a remarkable object lying half-hidden in one of those little borders of grass which edge the bases of vast legal buildings. He could only touch it with the point of his stick through the railings; but he could see that it was a piece of china of the most remarkable shape, as nearly resembling a starfish as anything—shaped, or broken accidentally, into five irregular but unmistakable points. The colouring was mainly blue, but green stripes or spots of some kind overlaid the blue, and lines of crimson gave it a richness and lustre of the most attractive kind. John was determined to possess it; but the more he pushed, the further it receded. At length he was forced to go back to his rooms and improvise a wire ring attached to the end of a stick, with which, by dint of great care and skill, he finally drew the piece of china within reach of his hands. As he seized hold of it he exclaimed in triumph. At that moment the clock struck. It was out of the question that he should keep his appointment. The meeting was held without him. But how had the piece of china been broken into this remarkable shape? A careful examination put it beyond doubt that the star shape was accidental, which made it all the more strange, and it seemed unlikely that there should be another such in existence. Set at the opposite end of the mantelpiece from the lump of glass that had been dug from the sand, it looked like a creature from another world—freakish and fantastic as a harlequin. It seemed to be pirouetting through space, winking light like a fitful star. The contrast between the china so vivid and alert, and the glass so mute and contemplative, fascinated him, and wondering and amazed he asked himself how the two came to exist in the same world, let alone to stand upon the same narrow strip of marble in the same room. The question remained unanswered.

He now began to haunt the places which are most prolific of broken china, such as pieces of waste land between railway lines, sites of demolished houses, and commons in the neighbourhood of London. But china is seldom thrown from a great height; it is one of the rarest of human actions. You have to find in conjunction a very high house, and a woman of such reckless impulse and passionate prejudice that she flings her jar or pot straight from the window without thought of who is below. Broken china was to be found in plenty, but broken in some trifling domestic accident, without purpose or character. Nevertheless, he was often astonished, as he came to go into the question more deeply, by the immense variety of shapes to be found in London alone, and there was still more cause for wonder and speculation in the differences of qualities and designs. The finest specimens he would bring home and place upon his mantelpiece, where, however, their duty was more and more of an ornamental nature, since papers needing a weight to keep them down became scarcer and scarcer.

He neglected his duties, perhaps, or discharged them absent-mindedly, or his constituents when they visited him were unfavourably impressed by the appearance of his mantelpiece. At any rate he was not elected to represent them in Parliament, and his friend Charles, taking it much to heart and hurrying to condole with him, found him so little cast down by the disaster that he could only suppose that it was too serious a matter for him to realize all at once.

In truth, John had been that day to Barnes Common, and there under a furse bush had found a very remarkable piece of iron. It was almost identical with the glass in shape, massy and globular, but so cold and heavy, so black and metallic, that it was evidently alien to the earth and had its origin in one of the dead stars or was itself the cinder of a moon. It weighed his pocket down; it weighed the mantelpiece down; it radiated cold. And yet the meteorite stood upon the same ledge with the lump of glass and the star-shaped china.

As his eyes passed from one to another, the determination to possess objects that even surpassed these tormented the young man. He devoted himself more and more resolutely to the search. If he had not been consumed by ambition and convinced that one day some newly-discovered rubbish heap would reward him, the disappointments he had suffered, let alone the fatigue and derision, would have made him give up the pursuit. Provided with a bag and a long stick fitted with an adaptable hook, he ransacked all deposits of earth; raked beneath matted tangles of scrub; searched all alleys and spaces between walls where he had learned to expect to find objects of this kind thrown away. As his standard became higher and his taste more severe the disappointments were innumerable, but always some gleam of hope, some piece of china or glass curiously marked or broken, lured him on. Day after day passed. He was no longer young. His career—that is his political career—was a thing of the past. People gave up visiting him. He was too silent to be worth asking to dinner. He never talked to anyone about his serious ambitions; their lack of understanding was apparent in their behaviour.

He leaned back in his chair now and watched Charles lift the stones on the mantelpiece a dozen times and put them down emphatically to mark what he was saying about the conduct of the Government, without once noticing their existence.

"What was the truth of it, John?" asked Charles suddenly, turning and facing him. "What made you give it up like that all in a second?"

"I've not given it up," John replied.

"But you've not the ghost of a chance now," said Charles roughly.

"I don't agree with you there," said John with conviction. Charles looked at him and was profoundly uneasy; the most extraordinary doubts possessed him; he had a queer sense that they were talking about different things. He looked round to find some relief for his horrible depression, but the disorderly appearance of the room depressed him still further. What was that stick, and the old carpet bag hanging against the wall? And then those stones? Looking at John, something fixed and distant in his expression alarmed him. He knew only too well that his mere appearance upon a platform was out of the question.

"Pretty stones," he said as cheerfully as he could; and saying that he had an appointment to keep, he left John—for ever.

The New Dress

Mabel had her first serious suspicion that something was wrong as she took her cloak off and Mrs. Barnet, while handing her the mirror and touching the brushes and thus drawing her attention, perhaps rather markedly, to all the appliances for tidying and improving hair, complexion, clothes, which existed on the dressing table, confirmed the suspicion,—that it was not right, not quite right, which growing stronger as she went upstairs and springing at her with conviction as she greeted Clarissa Dalloway, she went straight to the far end of the room, to a shaded corner where a looking-glass hung and looked. No! It was not *right*. And at once the misery which she always tried to hide, the profound dissatisfaction,—the sense she had had, ever since she was a child, of being inferior to other people,—set upon her, relentlessly, remorselessly, with an intensity which she could not beat off, as she would when she woke at night at home, by reading Borrow or Scott; for oh these men, oh these women, all were thinking,—"What's Mabel wearing? What a fright she looks! What a hideous new dress!"—their eyelids flickering as they came up and then their lids shutting rather tight. It was her own appalling inadequacy; her cowardice; her mean, water-sprinkled blood that depressed her. And at once the whole of the room where, for ever so many hours, she had planned with the little dressmaker how it was to go, seemed sordid, repulsive; and her own drawing-room so shabby, and herself, going out, puffed up with vanity as she touched the letters on the hall table and said: "How dull!" to show off,—all this now seemed unutterably silly, paltry, and provincial. All this had been absolutely destroyed, shown up, exploded, the moment she came into Mrs. Dalloway's drawing-room.

What she had thought that evening when, sitting over the teacups, Mrs. Dalloway's invitation came, was that, of course, she could not be fashionable. It was absurd to pretend it even,—fashion meant cut, meant style, meant thirty guineas at least,—but why not be original? Why not be herself, anyhow? And, getting up, she had taken that old fashion book of her mother's, a Paris fashion book of the time of the Empire, and had thought how much prettier, more dignified, and more womanly they were then, and so set herself,—oh, it was foolish,—trying to be like them, pluming herself in fact, upon being modest and old-fashioned and very charming, giving herself up, no doubt about it, to an orgy of self-love, which deserved to be chastised, and so rigged herself out like this.

But she dared not look in the glass. She could not face the whole horror,—the pale yellow, idiotically old-fashioned silk dress with its long skirt and its high sleeves and its waist and all the things that looked so charming in the fashion book, but not on her, not among all these ordinary people. She felt like a dressmaker's dummy standing there, for young people to stick pins into.

"But, my dear, it's perfectly charming!" Rose Shaw said, looking her up and down with that little satirical pucker of the lips which she expected,—Rose herself being dressed in the height of the fashion, precisely like everybody else, always.

We are all like flies trying to crawl over the edge of the saucer, Mabel thought, and repeated the phrase as if she were crossing herself, as if she were trying to find some spell to annul this pain, to make this agony endurable. Tags of Shakespeare, lines from books she had read ages ago, suddenly came to her when she was in agony, and she repeated them over and over again. "Flies trying to crawl," she repeated. If she could say that over often enough and make herself see the flies, she would become numb, chill, frozen, dumb. Now she could see flies crawling slowly out of a saucer of milk with their wings stuck together; and she strained and strained (standing in front of the looking-glass, listening to Rose Shaw) to make herself see Rose Shaw and all the other people there as flies, trying to hoist themselves out of something, or into something, meagre, insignificant, toiling flies. But she could not see them like that, not other people. She saw herself like that,—she was a fly, but the others were dragon-flies, butterflies, beautiful insects, dancing, fluttering, skimming, while she alone dragged herself up out of the saucer. (Envy and spite, the most detestable of the vices, were her chief faults.)

"I feel like some dowdy, decrepit, horribly dingy old fly," she said, making Robert Haydon stop just to hear her say that, just to reassure herself by furbishing up a poor weak-kneed phrase and so showing how detached she was, how witty, that she did not feel in the least out of anything. And, of course, Robert Haydon answered something quite polite, quite insincere, which she saw through instantly, and said to herself, directly he went, (again from some book), "Lies, lies, lies!" For a party makes things either much more real, or much less real, she thought; she saw in a flash to the bottom of Robert Haydon's heart; she saw through everything. She saw the truth. *This* was true, this drawing-room, this self, and the other false. Miss Milan's little workroom was really terribly hot, stuffy, sordid. It smelt of clothes and cabbage cooking; and yet, when Miss Milan put the glass in her hand, and she looked at herself with the dress on, finished, an extraordinary bliss shot through her heart. Suffused with light, she sprang into existence. Rid of cares and wrinkles, what she had dreamed of herself was there,—a beautiful woman. Just for a second (she had not dared look longer, Miss Milan wanted to know about the length of the skirt), there looked at her, framed in the scrolloping mahogany, a gray-white, mysteriously smiling, charming girl, the core of herself, the soul of herself; and it was not vanity only, not only self-love that made her think it good, tender, and true. Miss Milan said that the skirt could not well be longer; if anything the skirt, said Miss Milan, puckering her forehead, considering with all her wits about her, must be shorter; and she felt, suddenly, honestly, full of love for Miss Milan, much, much fonder of Miss Milan than of any one in the whole world, and could have cried for pity that she should be crawling on the floor with her mouth full of pins, and her face red and her eyes bulging,—that one human being should be doing this for another, and she saw them all as human beings merely, and herself going off to her party, and Miss Milan pulling the cover over the canary's cage, or letting him pick a hemp-seed from between her lips, and the thought of it, of this side of human nature and its patience and its endurance and its being content with such miserable, scanty, sordid, little pleasures filled her eyes with tears.

And now the whole thing had vanished. The dress, the room, the love, the pity, the scrolloping looking-glass, and the canary's cage,—all had vanished, and here she was in a corner of Mrs. Dalloway's drawing-room, suffering tortures, woken wide awake to reality.

But it was all so paltry, weak-blooded, and petty-minded to care so much at her age with two children, to be still so utterly dependent on people's opinions and not have principles or convictions, not to be able to say as other people did, "There's Shakespeare! There's death! We're all weevils in a captain's biscuit,"—or whatever it was that people did say.

She faced herself straight in the glass; she pecked at her left shoulder; she issued out into the room, as if spears were thrown at her yellow dress from all sides. But instead of looking fierce or tragic, as Rose Shaw would have done,—Rose would have looked like Boadicea,—she looked foolish and self-conscious, and simpered like a schoolgirl and slouched across the room, positively slinking, as if she were a beaten mongrel, and looked at a picture, an engraving. As if one went to a party to look at a picture! Everybody knew why she did it,—it was from shame, from humiliation.

"Now the fly's in the saucer," she said to herself, "right in the middle, and can't get out, and the milk," she thought, rigidly staring at the picture, "is sticking its wings together."

"It's so old-fashioned," she said to Charles Burt, making him stop (which by itself he hated) on his way to talk to some one else.

She meant, or she tried to make herself think that she meant, that it was the picture and not her dress, that was old-fashioned. And one word of praise, one word of affection from Charles would have made all the difference to her at the moment. If he had only said, "Mabel, you're looking charming to-night!" it would have changed her life. But then she ought to have been truthful and direct. Charles said nothing of the kind, of course. He was malice itself. He always saw through one, especially if one were feeling particularly mean, paltry, or feeble-minded.

"Mabel's got a new dress!" he said, and the poor fly was absolutely shoved into the middle of the saucer. Really, he would like her to drown, she believed. He had no heart, no fundamental kindness, only a veneer of friendliness. Miss Milan was much more real, much kinder. If only one could feel that and stick to it, always. "Why," she asked herself,—replying to Charles much too pertly, letting him see that she was out of temper, or "ruffled" as he called it ("Rather ruffled?" he said and went on to laugh at her with some woman over there),—"Why," she asked herself, "can't I feel one thing always, feel quite sure that Miss Milan is right, and Charles wrong and stick to it, feel sure about the canary and pity and love and not be whipped all round in a second by coming into a room full of people?" It was her odious, weak, vacillating character again, always giving at the critical moment and not being seriously interested in conchology, etymology, botany, archeology, cutting up potatoes and watching them fructify like Mary Dennis, like Violet Searle.

Then Mrs. Holman, seeing her standing there, bore down upon her. Of course a thing like a dress was beneath Mrs. Holman's notice, with her family always tumbling downstairs or having the scarlet fever. Could Mabel tell her if Elmthorpe was ever let for August and September? Oh, it was a conversation that bored her unutterably!—it made her furious to be treated like a house agent or a messenger boy, to be made use of. Not to have value, that was it, she thought, trying to grasp something hard, something real, while she tried to answer sensibly about the bathroom and the south aspect and the hot water to the top of the house; and all the time she could see little bits of her yellow dress in the round looking-glass which made them all the size of boot-buttons or tadpoles; and it was amazing to think how much humiliation and agony and self-loathing and effort and passionate ups and downs of feeling were contained in a thing the size of a three penny bit. And what was still odder, this thing, this Mabel Waring, was separate, quite disconnected; and though Mrs. Holman (the black button) was leaning forward and telling her how her eldest boy had strained his heart running, she could see her, too, quite detached in the looking-glass, and it was impossible that the black dot, leaning forward, gesticulating, should make the yellow dot, sitting solitary, self-centred, feel what the black dot was feeling, yet they pretended.

"So impossible to keep boys quiet,"—that was the kind of thing one said.

And Mrs. Holman, who could never get enough sympathy and snatched what little there was greedily, as if it were her right (but she deserved much more for there was her little girl who had come down this morning with a swollen knee-joint), took this miserable offering and looked at it suspiciously, grudgingly, as if it were a halfpenny when it ought to have been a pound and put it away in her purse, must put up with it, mean and miserly though it was, times being hard, so very hard; and on she went, creaking, injured Mrs. Holman, about the girl with the swollen joints. Ah, it was tragic, this greed, this clamor of human beings, like a row of cormorants, barking and flapping their wings for sympathy,—it was tragic, could one have felt it and not merely pretended to feel it!

But in her yellow dress to-night she could not wring out one drop more; she wanted it all, all for herself. She knew (she kept on looking into the glass, dipping into that dreadfully showing-up blue pool) that she was condemned, despised, left like this in a backwater, because of her being like this a feeble, vacillating creature; and it seemed to her that the yellow dress was a penance which she had deserved, and if she had been dressed like Rose Shaw, in lovely, clinging green with a ruffle of swansdown, she would have deserved that; and she thought that there was no escape for her,—none whatever. But it was not her fault altogether, after all. It was being one of a family of ten; never having money enough, always skimping and paring; and her mother carrying great cans, and the linoleum worn on the stair edges, and one sordid little domestic tragedy after another,—nothing catastrophic, the sheep farm failing, but not utterly; her eldest brother marrying beneath him but not very much,—there was no romance, nothing extreme about them all. They petered out respectably in seaside resorts; every watering-place had one of her aunts even now asleep in some lodging with the front windows not quite facing the sea. That was so like them,—they had to squint at things always. And she had done the same,—she was just like her aunts. For all her dreams of living in India, married to some hero like Sir Henry Lawrence, some empire builder (still the sight of a native in a turban filled her with romance), she had failed utterly. She had married Hubert, with his safe, permanent underling's job in the Law Courts, and they managed tolerably in a smallish house, without proper maids, and hash when she was alone or just bread and butter, but now and then,—Mrs. Holman was off, thinking her the most dried-up, unsympathetic twig she had ever met, absurdly dressed, too, and would tell every one about Mabel's fantastic appearance,—now and then, thought Mabel Waring, left alone on the blue sofa, punching the cushion in order to look occupied, for she would not join Charles Burt and Rose Shaw, chattering like magpies and perhaps laughing at her by the fireplace,—now and then, there did come to her delicious moments, reading the other night in bed, for instance, or down by the sea on the sand in the sun, at Easter,—let her recall it,—a great tuft of pale sand-grass standing all twisted like a shock of spears against the sky, which was blue like a smooth china egg, so firm, so hard, and then the melody of the waves,—"Hush, hush," they said, and the children's shouts paddling,—yes, it was a divine moment, and there she lay, she felt, in the hand of the Goddess who was the world; rather a hard-hearted, but very beautiful Goddess, a little lamb laid on the altar (one did think these silly things, and it didn't matter so long as one never said them). And also with Hubert sometimes she had quite unexpectedly,—carving the mutton for Sunday lunch, for no reason, opening a letter, coming into a room,—divine moments, when she said to herself (for she would never say this to anybody else), "This is it. This has happened. This is it!" And the other way about it was equally surprising,—that is, when everything was arranged,—music, weather, holidays, every reason for happiness was there,—then nothing happened at all. One wasn't happy. It was flat, just flat, that was all.

Her wretched self again, no doubt! She had always been a fretful, weak, unsatisfactory mother, a wobbly wife, lolling about in a kind of twilight existence with nothing very clear or very bold or more one thing than another, like all her brothers and sisters, except perhaps Herbert,—they were all the same poor water-veined creatures who did nothing. Then in the midst of this creeping, crawling life, suddenly she was on the crest of a wave. That wretched fly,—where had she read the story that kept coming into her mind about the fly and the saucer?—struggled out. Yes, she had those moments. But now that she was forty, they might come more and more seldom. By degrees she would cease to struggle any more. But that was deplorable! That was not to be endured! That made her feel ashamed of herself!

She would go to the London Library to-morrow. She would find some wonderful, helpful, astonishing book, quite by chance, a book by a clergyman, by an American no one had ever heard of; or she would walk down the Strand and drop, accidentally, into a hall where a miner was telling about the life in the pit and suddenly she would become a new person. She would be absolutely transformed. She would wear a uniform; she would be called Sister Somebody; she would never give a thought to clothes again. And for ever after she would be perfectly clear about Charles Burt and Miss Milan and this room and that room; and it would be always, day after day, as if she were lying in the sun or carving the mutton. It would be it!

So she got up from the blue sofa, and the yellow button in the looking-glass got up too, and she waved her hand to Charles and Rose to show them she did not depend on them one scrap, and the yellow button moved out of the looking-glass, and all the spears were gathered into her breast as she walked towards Mrs. Dalloway and said, "Good night."

"But it's too early to go," said Mrs. Dalloway, who was always so charming.

"I'm afraid I must," said Mabel Waring. "But," she

added in her weak, wobbly voice which only sounded ridiculous when she tried to strengthen it, "I have enjoyed myself enormously."

"I have enjoyed myself," she said to Mr. Dalloway, whom she met on the stairs.

"Lies, lies, lies!" she said to herself, going downstairs, and "Right in the saucer!" she said to herself as she thanked Mrs. Barnet for helping her and wrapped herself, round and round and round, in the Chinese cloak she had worn these twenty years.

An Unwritten Novel

Such an expression of unhappiness was enough by itself to make one's eyes slide above the paper's edge to the poor woman's face—insignificant without that look, almost a symbol of human destiny with it. Life's what you see in people's eyes; life's what they learn, and, having learnt it, never, though they seek to hide it, cease to be aware of—what? That life's like that, it seems. Five faces opposite—five mature faces—and the knowledge in each face. Strange, though, how people want to conceal it! Marks of reticence are on all those faces: lips shut, eyes shaded, each one of the five doing something to hide or stultify his knowledge. One smokes; another reads; a third checks entries in a pocket book; a fourth stares at the map of the line framed opposite; and the fifth—the terrible thing about the fifth is that she does nothing at all. She looks at life. Ah, but my poor, unfortunate woman, do play the game—do, for all our sakes, conceal it!

As if she heard me, she looked up, shifted slightly in her seat and sighed. She seemed to apologise and at the same time to say to me, "If only you knew!" Then she looked at life again. "But I do know," I answered silently, glancing at the *Times* for manners' sake: "I know the whole business. 'Peace between Germany and the Allied Powers was yesterday officially ushered in at Paris—Signor Nitti, the Italian Prime Minister—a passenger train at Doncaster was in collision with a goods train . . .' We all know—the *Times* knows—but we pretend we don't." My eyes had once more crept over the paper's rim. She shuddered, twitched her arm queerly to the middle of her back and shook her head. Again I dipped into my great reservoir of life. "Take what you like," I continued, "births, deaths, marriages, Court Circular, the habits of birds, Leonardo da Vinci, the Sandhills murder, high wages and the cost of living—oh, take what you like," I repeated, "it's all in the *Times!*" Again with infinite weariness she moved her head from side to side until, like a top exhausted with spinning, it settled on her neck.

The *Times* was no protection against such sorrow as hers. But other human beings forbade intercourse. The best thing to do against life was to fold the paper so that it made a perfect square, crisp, thick, impervious even to life. This done, I glanced up quickly, armed with a shield of my own. She pierced through my shield; she gazed into my eyes as if searching any sediment of courage at the depths of them and damping it to clay. Her twitch alone denied all hope, discounted all illusion.

So we rattled through Surrey and across the border into Sussex. But with my eyes upon life I did not see that the other travellers had left, one by one, till, save for the man who read, we were alone together. Here was Three Bridges station. We drew slowly down the platform and stopped. Was he going to leave us? I prayed both ways—I prayed last that he might stay. At that instant he roused himself, crumpled his paper contemptuously, like a thing done with, burst open the door and left us alone.

The unhappy woman, leaning a little forward, palely and colourlessly addressed me—talked of stations and holidays, of brothers at Eastbourne, and the time of year, which was, I forget now, early or late. But at last looking from the window and seeing, I knew, only life, she breathed, "Staying away—that's the drawback of it——" Ah, now we approached the catastrophe, "My sister-in-law"—the bitterness of her tone was like lemon on cold steel, and speaking, not to me, but to herself, she muttered, "Nonsense, she would say—that's what they all say," and while she spoke she fidgeted as though the skin on her back were as a plucked fowl's in a poulterer's shop-window.

"Oh that cow!" she broke off nervously, as though the great wooden cow in the meadow had shocked her and saved her from some indiscretion. Then she shuddered, and then she made the awkward angular movement that I had seen before, as if, after the spasm, some spot between the shoulders burnt or itched. Then again she looked the most unhappy woman in the world, and I once more reproached her, though not with the same conviction, for if there were a reason, and if I knew the reason, the stigma was removed from life.

"Sisters-in-law," I said—

Her lips pursed as if to spit venom at the word; pursed they remained. All she did was to take her glove and rub hard at a spot on the window-pane. She rubbed as if she would rub something out for ever—some stain, some indelible contamination. Indeed, the spot remained for all her rubbing, and back she sank with the shudder and the clutch of the arm I had come to expect. Something impelled me to take my glove and rub my window. There, too, was a little speck on the glass. For all my rubbing it remained. And then the spasm went through me; I crooked my arm and plucked at the middle of my back. My skin, too, felt like the damp chicken's skin in the poulterer's shop window; one spot between the shoulders itched and irritated, felt clammy, felt raw. Could I reach it? Surreptitiously I tried. She saw me. A smile of infinite irony, infinite sorrow, flitted and faded from her face. But she had communicated, shared her secret, passed her poison; she would speak no more. Leaning back in my corner, shielding my eyes from her eyes, seeing only the slopes and hollows, greys and purples, of the winter's landscape, I read her message, deciphered her secret, reading it beneath her gaze.

Hilda's the sister-in-law. Hilda? Hilda? Hilda Marsh—Hilda the blooming, the full bosomed, the matronly. Hilda stands at the door as the cab draws up, holding a coin. "Poor Minnie, more of a grasshopper than ever—old cloak she had last year. Well, well, with two children these days one can't do more. No, Minnie, I've got it; here you are, cabby—none of your ways with me. Come in, Minnie. Oh, I could carry *you*, let alone your basket!" So they go into the dining-room. "Aunt Minnie, children."

Slowly the knives and forks sink from the upright. Down they get (Bob and Barbara), hold out hands stiffly; back again to their chairs, staring between the resumed mouthfuls. [But this we'll skip; ornaments, curtains, trefoil china plate, yellow oblongs of cheese, white squares of biscuit—skip—oh, but wait! Half-way through luncheon one of those shivers; Bob stares at her, spoon in mouth. "Get on with your pudding, Bob;" but Hilda disapproves. "Why *should* she twitch?" Skip, skip, till we reach the landing on the upper floor; stairs brass-bound; linoleum worn; oh, yes! little bedroom looking out over the roofs of Eastbourne—zigzagging roofs like the spines of caterpillars, this way, that way, striped red and yellow, with blue-black slating]. Now, Minnie, the door's shut; Hilda heavily descends to the basement; you unstrap the straps of your basket, lay on the bed a meagre nightgown, stand side by side furred felt slippers. The looking-glass—no, you avoid the looking-glass. Some methodical disposition of hat-pins. Perhaps the shell box has something in it? You shake it; it's the pearl stud there was last year—that's all. And then the sniff, the sigh, the sitting by the window. Three o'clock on a December afternoon; the rain drizzling; one light low in the skylight of a drapery emporium; another high in a servant's bedroom—this one goes out. That gives her nothing to look at. A moment's blankness—then, what are you thinking? (Let me peep across at her opposite; she's asleep or pretending it; so what would she think about sitting at the window at three o'clock in the afternoon? Health, money, hills, her God?) Yes, sitting on the very edge of the chair looking over the roofs of Eastbourne, Minnie Marsh prays to God. That's all very well; and she may rub the pane too, as though to see God better; but what God does she see? Who's the God of Minnie Marsh, the God of the back streets of Eastbourne, the God of the three o'clock in the afternoon? I, too, see roofs, I see sky; but, oh, dear—this seeing of Gods! More like President Kruger than Prince Albert—that's the best I can do for him; and I see him on a chair, in a black frock-coat, not so very high up either; I can manage a cloud or two for him to sit on; and then his hand trailing in the cloud holds a rod, a truncheon is it?—black, thick, thorned—a brutal old bully—Minnie's God! Did he send the itch and the patch and the twitch? Is that why she prays? What she rubs on the window is the stain of sin. Oh, she committed some crime!

I have my choice of crimes. The woods flit and fly—in summer there are bluebells; in the opening there, when Spring comes, primroses. A parting, was it, twenty years ago? Vows broken? Not Minnie's! . . . She was faithful. How she nursed her mother! All her savings on the tombstone—wreaths under glass—daffodils in jars. But I'm off the track. A crime. . . . They would say she kept her sorrow, suppressed her secret—her sex, they'd say—the scientific people. But what flummery to saddle *her* with sex! No—more like this. Passing down the streets of Croydon twenty years ago, the violet loops of ribbon in the draper's window spangled in the electric light catch her eye. She lingers—past six. Still by running she can reach home. She pushes through the glass swing door. It's sale-time. Shallow trays brim with ribbons. She pauses, pulls this, fingers that with the raised roses on it—no need to choose, no need to buy, and each tray with its surprises. "We don't shut till seven," and then it *is* seven. She runs, she rushes, home she reaches, but too late. Neighbours—the doctor—baby brother—the kettle—scalded—hospital—dead—or only the shock of it, the blame? Ah, but the detail matters nothing! It's what she carries with her; the spot, the crime, the thing to expiate, always there between her shoulders. "Yes," she seems to nod to me, "it's the thing I did."

Whether you did, or what you did, I don't mind; it's not the thing I want. The draper's window looped with violet—that'll do; a little cheap perhaps, a little commonplace—since one has a choice of crimes, but then so many (let me peep across again—still sleeping, or pretending sleep! white, worn, the mouth closed—a touch of obstinacy, more than one would think—no hint of sex)—so many crimes aren't *your* crime; your crime was cheap; only the retribution solemn; for now the church door opens, the hard wooden pew receives her; on the brown tiles she kneels; every day, winter, summer, dusk, dawn (here she's at it) prays. All her sins fall, fall, for ever fall. The spot receives them. It's raised, it's red, it's burning. Next she twitches. Small boys point. "Bob at lunch to-day"—But elderly women are the worst.

Indeed now you can't sit praying any longer. Kruger's sunk beneath the clouds—washed over as with a painter's brush of liquid grey, to which he adds a tinge of black—even the tip of the truncheon gone now. That's what always happens! Just as you've seen him, felt him, someone interrupts. It's Hilda now.

How you hate her! She'll even lock the bathroom door overnight, too, though it's only cold water you want, and sometimes when the night's been bad it seems as if washing helped. And John at breakfast—the children—meals are worst, and sometimes there are friends—ferns don't altogether hide 'em—they guess too; so out you go along the front, where the waves are grey, and the papers blow, and the glass shelters green and draughty, and the chairs cost tuppence—too much—for there must be preachers along the sands. Ah, that's a funny man—that's a man with parakeets—poor little creatures! Is there no one here who thinks of God?—just up there, over the pier, with his rod—but no—there's nothing but grey in the sky or if it's blue the white clouds hide him, and the music—it's military music—and what are they fishing for? Do they catch them? How the children stare! Well, then home a back way—"Home a back way!" The words have meaning; might have been spoken by the old man with whiskers—no, no, he didn't really speak; but everything has meaning—placards leaning against doorways—names above shop-windows—red fruit in baskets—women's heads in the hairdresser's—all say "Minnie Marsh!" But here's a jerk, "Eggs are cheaper!" That's what always happens! I was heading her over the waterfall, straight for madness, when, like a flock of dream sheep, she turns t'other way and runs between my fingers. Eggs are cheaper. Tethered to the shores of the world, none of the crimes, sorrows, rhapsodies, or insanities for poor Minnie Marsh; never late for luncheon; never caught in a storm without a mackintosh; never utterly unconscious of the cheapness of eggs. So she reaches home—scrapes her boots.

Have I read you right? But the human face—the human face at the top of the fullest sheet of print holds more, withholds more. Now, eyes open, she looks out; and in the human eye—how d'you define it?—there's a break—a division—so that when you've grasped the stem the butterfly's off—the moth that hangs in the evening over the yellow flower—move, raise your hand, off, high, away. I won't raise my hand. Hang still, then, quiver, life, soul, spirit, whatever you are of Minnie Marsh—I, too, on my flower—the hawk over the down—alone, or what were the worth of life? To rise; hang still in the evening, in the midday; hang still over the down. The flicker of a hand—off, up! then poised again. Alone, unseen; seeing all so still down there, all so lovely. None seeing, none caring. The eyes of others our prisons; their thoughts our cages. Air above, air below. And the moon and immortality . . . Oh, but I drop to the turf! Are you down too, you in the corner, what's your name—woman—Minnie Marsh; some such name as that? There she is, tight to her blossom; opening her hand-bag, from which she takes a hollow shell—an egg—who was saying that eggs were cheaper? You or I? Oh, it was you who said it on the way home, you remember, when the old gentleman, suddenly opening his umbrella—or sneezing was it? Anyhow, Kruger went, and you came "home a back way," and scraped your boots. Yes. And now you lay across your knees a pocket-handkerchief into which drop little angular fragments of eggshell—fragments of a map—a puzzle. I wish I could piece them together! If you would only sit still. She's moved her knees—the map's in bits again. Down the slopes of the Andes the white blocks of marble go bounding and hurtling, crushing to death a whole troop of Spanish muleteers, with their convoy—Drake's booty, gold and silver. But to return——

To what, to where? She opened the door, and, putting her umbrella in the stand—that goes without saying; so, too, the whiff of beef from the basement; dot, dot, dot. But what I cannot thus eliminate, what I must, head down, eyes shut, with the courage of a battalion and the blindness of a bull, charge and disperse are, indubitably, the figures behind the ferns, commercial travellers. There I've hidden them all this time in the hope that somehow they'd disappear, or better still emerge, as indeed they must, if the story's to go on gathering richness and rotundity, destiny and tragedy, as stories should, rolling along with it two, if not three, commercial travellers and a whole grove of aspidistra. "The fronds of the aspidistra only partly concealed the commercial traveller—" Rhododendrons would conceal him utterly, and into the bargain give me my fling of red and white, for which I starve and strive; but rhododendrons in Eastbourne—in December—on the Marshes' table—no, no, I dare not; it's all a matter of crusts and cruets, frills and ferns. Perhaps there'll be a moment later by the sea. Moreover, I feel, pleasantly pricking through the green fretwork and over the glacis of cut glass, a desire to peer and peep at the man opposite—one's as much as I can manage. James Moggridge is it, whom the Marshes call Jimmy? [Minnie you must promise not to twitch till I've got this straight]. James Moggridge travels in—shall we say buttons?—but the time's not come for bringing *them* in—the big and the little on the long cards, some peacock-eyed, others dull gold; cairngorms some, and others coral sprays—but I say the time's not come. He travels, and on Thursdays, his Eastbourne day, takes his meals with the Marshes. His red face, his little steady eyes—by no means altogether commonplace—his enormous appetite (that's safe; he won't look at Minnie till the bread's swamped the gravy dry), napkin tucked diamond-wise—but this is primitive, and, whatever it may do the reader, don't take me in. Let's dodge to the Moggridge household, set that in motion. Well, the family boots are mended on Sundays by James himself. He reads *Truth*. But his passion? Roses—and his wife a retired hospital nurse—interesting—for God's sake let me have one woman with a name I like! But no; she's of the unborn children of the mind, illicit, none the less loved, like my rhododendrons. How many die in every novel that's written—the best, the dearest, while Moggridge lives. It's life's fault. Here's Minnie eating her egg at the moment opposite and at t'other end of the line—are we past Lewes?—there must be Jimmy—or what's her twitch for?

There must be Moggridge—life's fault. Life imposes her laws; life blocks the way; life's behind the fern; life's the tyrant; oh, but not the bully! No, for I assure you I come willingly; I come wooed by Heaven knows what compulsion across ferns and cruets, table splashed and bottles smeared. I come irresistibly to lodge myself somewhere on the firm flesh, in the robust spine, wherever I can penetrate or find foothold on the person, in the soul, of Moggridge the man. The enormous stability of the fabric; the spine tough as whalebone, straight as oak-tree; the ribs radiating branches; the flesh taut tarpaulin; the red hollows; the suck and regurgitation of the heart; while from above meat falls in brown cubes and beer gushes to be churned to blood again—and so we reach the eyes. Behind the aspidistra they see something: black, white, dismal; now the plate again; behind the aspidistra they see elderly woman; "Marsh's sister, Hilda's more my sort;" the tablecloth now. "Marsh would know what's wrong with Morrises . . ." talk that over; cheese has come; the plate again; turn it round—the enormous fingers; now the woman opposite. "Marsh's sister—not a bit like Marsh; wretched elderly female. . . . You should feed your hens. . . . God's truth, what's set her twitching? Not what *I* said? Dear, dear, dear! these elderly women. Dear, dear!"

[Yes, Minnie; I know you've twitched, but one moment—James Moggridge].

"Dear, dear, dear!" How beautiful the sound is! like the knock of a mallet on seasoned timber, like the throb of the heart of an ancient whaler when the seas press thick and the green is clouded. 'Dear, dear!' what a passing bell for the souls of the fretful to soothe them and solace them, lap them in linen, saying, "So long. Good luck to you!" and then, "What's your pleasure?" for though Moggridge would pluck his rose for her, that's done, that's over. Now what's the next thing? "Madam, you'll miss your train," for they don't linger.

That's the man's way; that's the sound that reverberates; that's St. Paul's and the motor-omnibuses. But we're brushing the crumbs off. Oh, Moggridge, you won't stay? You must be off? Are you driving through Eastbourne this afternoon in one of those little carriages? Are you the man who's walled up in green cardboard boxes, and sometimes has the blinds down, and sometimes sits so solemn staring like a sphinx, and always there's a look of the sepulchral, something of the undertaker, the coffin, and the dusk about horse and driver? Do tell me—but the doors slammed. We shall never meet again. Moggridge, farewell!

Yes, yes, I'm coming. Right up to the top of the house. One moment I'll linger. How the mud goes round in the mind—what a swirl these monsters leave, the waters rocking, the weeds waving and green here, black there, striking to the sand, till by degrees the atoms reassemble, the deposit sifts itself, and again through the eyes one sees clear and still, and there comes to the lips some prayer for the departed, some obsequy for the souls of those one nods to, the people one never meets again.

James Moggridge is dead now, gone for ever. Well, Minnie—"I can face it no longer." If she said that—(Let me look at her. She is brushing the eggshell into deep declivities). She said it certainly, leaning against the wall of the bedroom, and plucking at the little balls which edge the claret-coloured curtain. But when the self speaks to the self, who is speaking?—the entombed soul, the spirit driven in, in, in to the central catacomb; the self that took the veil and left the world—a coward perhaps, yet somehow beautiful, as it flits with its lantern restlessly up and down the dark corridors. "I can bear it no longer," her spirit says. "That man at lunch—Hilda—the children." Oh, heavens, her sob! It's the spirit wailing its destiny, the spirit driven hither, thither, lodging on the diminishing carpets—meagre footholds—shrunken shreds of all the vanishing universe—love, life, faith, husband, children, I know not what splendours and pageantries glimpsed in girlhood. "Not for me—not for me."

But then—the muffins, the bald elderly dog? Bead mats I should fancy and the consolation of underlinen. If Minnie Marsh were run over and taken to hospital, nurses and doctors themselves would exclaim. . . . There's the vista and the vision—there's the distance—the blue blot at the end of the avenue, while, after all, the tea is rich, the muffin hot, and the dog—"Benny, to your basket, sir, and see what mother's brought you!" So, taking the glove with the worn thumb, defying once more the encroaching demon of what's called going in holes, you renew the fortifications, threading the grey wool, running it in and out.

Running it in and out, across and over, spinning a web through which God himself—hush, don't think of God! How firm the stitches are! You must be proud of your darning. Let nothing disturb her. Let the light fall gently, and the clouds show an inner vest of the first green leaf. Let the sparrow perch on the twig and shake the raindrop hanging to the twig's elbow . . . Why look up? Was it a sound, a thought? Oh, heavens! Back again to the thing you did, the plate glass with the violet loops? But Hilda will come. Ignominies, humiliations, oh! Close the breach.

Having mended her glove, Minnie Marsh lays it in the drawer. She shuts the drawer with decision. I catch sight of her face in the glass. Lips are pursed. Chin held high. Next she laces her shoes. Then she touches her throat. What's your brooch? Mistletoe or merry-thought? And what is happening? Unless I'm much mistaken, the pulse's quickened, the moments coming, the threads are racing, Niagara's ahead. Here's the crisis! Heaven be with you! Down she goes. Courage, courage! Face it, be it! For God's sake don't wait on the mat now! There's the door! I'm on your side. Speak! Confront her, confound her soul!

"Oh, I beg your pardon! Yes, this is Eastbourne. I'll reach it down for you. Let me try the handle." [But, Minnie, though we keep up pretences, I've read you right—I'm with you now].

"That's all your luggage?"

"Much obliged, I'm sure."

(But why do you look about you? Hilda won't come to the station, nor John; and Moggridge is driving at the far side of Eastbourne).

"I'll wait by my bag, ma'am, that's safest. He said he'd meet me. . . . Oh, there he is! That's my son."

So they walk off together.

Well, but I'm confounded. . . . Surely Minnie, you know better! A strange young man. . . . Stop! I'll tell him—Minnie!—Miss Marsh!—I don't know though. There's something queer in her cloak as it blows. Oh, but it's untrue, it's indecent. . . . Look how he bends as they reach the gateway. She finds her ticket. What's the joke? Off they go, down the road, side by side. . . . Well, my world's done for! What do I stand on? What do I know? That's not Minnie. There never was Moggridge. Who am I? Life's bare as bone.

And yet the last look of them—he stepping from

the kerb and she following him round the edge of the big building brims me with wonder—floods me anew. Mysterious figures! Mother and son. Who are you? Why do you walk down the street? Where to-night will you sleep, and then, to-morrow? Oh, how it whirls and surges—floats me afresh! I start after them. People drive this way and that. The white light splutters and pours. Plate-glass windows. Carnations; chrysanthemums. Ivy in dark gardens. Milk carts at the door. Wherever I go, mysterious figures, I see you, turning the corner, mothers and sons; you, you, you. I hasten, I follow. This, I fancy, must be the sea. Grey is the landscape; dim as ashes; the water murmurs and moves. If I fall on my knees, if I go through the ritual, the ancient antics, it's you, unknown figures, you I adore; if I open my arms, it's you I embrace, you I draw to me—adorable world!

The Lady in the Looking-Glass

A Reflection

People should not leave looking-glasses hanging in their rooms any more than they should leave open check books or letters confessing some hideous crime. One could not help looking, that summer afternoon, in the long glass that hung outside in the hall. Chance had so arranged it. From the depths of the sofa in the drawing-room one could see reflected in the Italian glass not only the marble-topped table opposite, but a stretch of the garden beyond. One could see a long grass path leading between banks of tall flowers until, slicing off an angle, the gold rim cut it off.

The house was empty, and one felt, since one was the only person in the drawing-room, like one of those naturalists who, covered with grass and leaves, lie watching the shyest animals—badgers, otters, kingfishers—moving about freely, themselves unseen. The room that afternoon was full of such shy creatures, lights and shadows, curtains blowing, petals falling—things that never happen, so it seems, if someone is looking. The quiet old country room with its rugs and stone chimney pieces, its sunken book-cases and red and gold lacquer cabinets, was full of such nocturnal creatures. They came pirouetting across the floor, stepping delicately with high-lifted feet and spread tails and pecking allusive beaks as if they had been cranes or flocks of elegant flamingoes whose pink was faded, or peacocks whose trains were veiled with silver. And there were obscure flushes and darkenings too, as if a cuttlefish had suddenly suffused the air with purple; and the room had its passions and rages and envies and sorrows coming over it and clouding it, like a human being. Nothing stayed the same for two seconds together.

But, outside, the looking-glass reflected the hall table, the sunflowers, the garden path so accurately and so fixedly that they seemed held there in their reality unescapably. It was a strange contrast—all changing here, all stillness there. One could not help looking from one to the other. Meanwhile, since all the doors and windows were open in the heat, there was a perpetual sighing and ceasing sound, the voice of the transient and the perishing, it seemed, coming and going like human breath, while in the looking-glass things had ceased to breathe and lay still in the trance of immortality.

Half an hour ago the mistress of the house, Isabella Tyson, had gone down the grass path in her thin summer dress, carrying a basket, and had vanished, sliced off by the gilt rim of the looking-glass. She had gone presumably into the lower garden to pick flowers; or as it seemed more natural to suppose, to pick something light and fantastic and leafy and trailing, travelers' joy, or one of those elegant sprays of convolvulus that twine round ugly walls and burst here and there into white and violet blossoms. She suggested the fantastic and the tremulous convolvulus rather than the upright aster, the starched zinnia, or her own burning roses alight like lamps on the straight posts of their rose trees. The comparison showed how very little, after all these years, one knew about her; for it is impossible that any woman of flesh and blood of fifty-five or sixty should be really a wreath or a tendril. Such comparisons are worse than idle and superficial—they are cruel even, for they come like the convolvulus itself trembling between one's eyes and the truth. There must be truth; there must be a wall. Yet it was strange that after knowing her all these years one could not say what the truth about Isabella was; one still made up phrases like this about convolvulus and travelers' joy. As for facts, it was a fact that she was a spinster; that she was rich; that she had bought this house and collected with her own hands—often in the most obscure corners of the world and at great risk from poisonous stings and Oriental diseases—the rugs, the chairs, the cabinets which now lived their nocturnal life before one's eyes. Sometimes it seemed as if they knew more about her than we, who sat on them, wrote at them, and trod on them so carefully were allowed to know. In each of these cabinets were many little drawers, and each almost certainly held letters, tied with bows of ribbon, sprinkled with sticks of lavender or rose leaves. For it was another fact—if facts were what one wanted—that Isabella had known many people, had had many friends; and thus if one had the audacity to open a drawer and read her letters, one would find the traces of many agitations, of appointments to meet, of upbraidings for not having met, long letters of intimacy and affection, violent letters of jealousy and reproach, terrible final words of parting—for all those interviews and assignations had led to nothing—that is, she had never married, and yet, judging from the masklike indifference of her face, she had gone through twenty times more of passion and experience than those whose loves are trumpeted forth for all the world to hear. Under the stress of thinking about Isabella, her room became more shadowy and symbolic; the corners seemed darker, the legs of chairs and tables more spindly and hieroglyphic.

Suddenly these reflections were ended violently and yet without a sound. A large black form loomed into the looking-glass; blotted out everything, strewed the table with a packet of marble tablets veined with pink and gray, and was gone. But the picture was entirely altered. For the moment it was unrecognizable and irrational and entirely out of focus. One could not relate these tablets to any human purpose. And then by degrees some logical process set to work on them and began ordering and arranging them and bringing them into the fold of common experience. One realized at last that they were merely letters. The man had brought the post.

There they lay on the marble-topped table, all dripping with light and color at first and crude and unabsorbed. And then it was strange to see how they were drawn in and arranged and composed and made part of the picture and granted that stillness and immortality which the looking-glass conferred. They lay there invested with a new reality and significance and with a greater heaviness too, as if it would have needed a chisel to dislodge them from the table. And, whether it was fancy or not, they seemed to have become not merely a handful of casual letters but to be tablets graven with eternal truth—if one could read them, one would know everything there was to be known about Isabella, yes, and about life too. The pages inside those marble-looking envelopes must be cut deep and scored thick with meaning. Isabella would come in, and take them, one by one, very slowly, and open them, and read them carefully word by word, and then with a profound sigh of comprehension, as if she had seen to the bottom of everything, she would tear the envelopes to little bits and tie the letters together and lock the cabinet drawer in her determination to conceal what she did not wish to be known.

The thought served as a challenge. Isabella did not wish to be known—but she should no longer escape. It was absurd, it was monstrous. If she concealed so much and knew so much one must prize her open with the first tool that came to hand—the imagination. One must fix one's mind upon her at that very moment. One must fasten her down there. One must refuse to be put off any longer with sayings and doings such as the moment brought forth—with dinners and visits and polite conversations. One must put oneself in her shoes. If one took the phrase literally, it was easy to see the shoes in which she stood, down in the lower garden, at this moment. They were very narrow and long and fashionable—they were made of the softest and most flexible leather. Like everything she wore, they were exquisite. And she would be standing under the high hedge in the lower part of the garden, raising the scissors that were tied to her waist to cut some dead flower, some overgrown branch. The sun would beat down on her face, into her eyes; but no, at the critical moment a veil of cloud covered the sun, making the expression of her eyes doubtful—was it mocking or tender, brilliant or dull? One could only see the indeterminate outline of her rather faded, fine face looking at the sky. She was thinking, perhaps, that she must order a new net for the strawberries; that she must send flowers to Johnson's widow; that it was time she drove over to see the Hippesleys in their new house. Those were the things she talked about at dinner certainly. But one was tired of the things that she talked about at dinner. It was her profounder state of being that one wanted to catch and turn to words, the state that is to the mind what breathing is to the body, what one calls happiness or unhappiness. At the mention of those words it became obvious, surely, that she must be happy. She was rich; she was distinguished; she had many friends; she traveled—she bought rugs in Turkey and blue pots in Persia. Avenues of pleasure radiated this way and that from where she stood with her scissors raised to cut the trembling branches while the lacy clouds veiled her face.

Here with a quick movement of her scissors she snipped the spray of travelers' joy and it fell to the ground. As it fell, surely some light came in too, surely one could penetrate a little farther into her being. Her mind then was filled with tenderness and regret. . . . To cut an overgrown branch saddened her because it had once lived, and life was dear to her. Yes, and at the same time the fall of the branch would suggest to her how she must die herself and all the futility and evanescence of things. And then again quickly catching this thought up, with her instant good sense, she thought life had treated her well; even if fall she must, it was to lie on the earth and molder sweetly into the roots of violets. So she stood thinking. Without making any thought precise—for she was one of those reticent people whose minds hold their thoughts enmeshed in clouds of silence—she was filled with thoughts. Her mind was like her room, in which lights advanced and retreated, came pirouetting and stepping delicately, spread their tails, pecked their way; and then her whole being was suffused, like the room again, with a cloud of some profound knowledge, some unspoken regret, and then she was full of locked drawers, stuffed with letters, like her cabinets. To talk of "prizing her open" as if she were an oyster, to use any but the finest and subtlest and most pliable tools upon her was impious and absurd. One must imagine—here was she in the looking-glass. It made one start.

She was so far off at first that one could not see her clearly. She came lingering and pausing, here straightening a rose, there lifting a pink to smell it, but she never stopped; and all the time she became larger and larger in the looking-glass, more and more completely the person into whose mind one had been trying to penetrate. One verified her by degrees—fitted the qualities one had discovered into this visible body. There were her gray-green dress, and her long shoes, her basket, and something sparkling at her throat. She came so gradually that she did not seem to derange the pattern in the glass, but only to bring in some new element which gently moved and altered the other objects as if asking them, courteously, to make room for her. And the letters and the table and the grass walk and the sunflowers which had been waiting in the looking-glass separated and opened out so that she might be received among them. At last there she was, in the hall. She stopped dead. She stood by the table. She stood perfectly still. At once the looking-glass began to pour over her a light that seemed to fix her; that seemed like some acid to bite off the unessential and superficial and to leave only the truth. It was an enthralling spectacle. Everything dropped from her—clouds, dress, basket, diamond—all that one had called the creeper and convolvulus. Here was the hard wall beneath. Here was the woman herself. She stood naked in that pitiless light. And there was nothing. Isabella was perfectly empty. She had no thoughts. She had no friends. She cared for nobody. As for her letters, they were all bills. Look, as she stood there, old and angular, veined and lined, with her high nose and her wrinkled neck, she did not even trouble to open them.

People should not leave looking-glasses hanging in their rooms.

The Mark on the Wall

Perhaps it was the middle of January in the present year that I first looked up and saw the mark on the wall. In order to fix a date it is necessary to remember what one saw. So now I think of the fire; the steady film of yellow light upon the page of my book; the three chrysanthemums in the round glass bowl on the mantelpiece. Yes, it must have been the winter time, and we had just finished our tea, for I remember that I was smoking a cigarette when I looked up and saw the mark on the wall for the first time. I looked up through the smoke of my cigarette and my eye lodged for a moment upon the burning coals, and that old fancy of the crimson flag flapping from the castle tower came into my mind, and I thought of the cavalcade of red knights riding up the side of the black rock. Rather to my relief the sight of the mark interrupted the fancy, for it is an old fancy, an automatic fancy, made as a child perhaps. The mark was a small round mark, black upon the white wall, about six or seven inches above the mantelpiece.

How readily our thoughts swarm upon a new object, lifting it a little way, as ants carry a blade of straw so feverishly, and then leave it. . . . If that mark was made by a nail, it can't have been for a picture, it must have been for a miniature—the miniature of a lady with white powdered curls, powder-dusted cheeks, and lips like red carnations. A fraud of course, for the people who had this house before us would have chosen pictures in that way—an old picture for an old room. That is the sort of people they were—very interesting people, and I think of them so often, in such queer places, because one will never see them again, never know what happened next. They wanted to leave this house because they wanted to change their style of furniture, so he said, and he was in process of saying that in his opinion art should have ideas behind it when we were torn asunder, as one is torn from the old lady about to pour out tea and the young man about to hit the tennis ball in the back garden of the suburban villa as one rushes past in the train.

But as for that mark, I'm not sure about it; I don't believe it was made by a nail after all; it's too big, too round, for that. I might get up, but if I got up and looked at it, ten to one I shouldn't be able to say for certain; because once a thing's done, no one ever knows how it happened. O dear me, the mystery of life! The inaccuracy of thought! The ignorance of humanity! To show how very little control of our possessions we have—what an accidental affair this living is after all our civilization—let me just count over a few of the things lost in one lifetime, beginning, for that seems always the most mysterious of losses—what cat would gnaw, what rat would nibble—three pale blue canisters of book-binding tools? Then there were the bird cages, the iron hoops, the steel skates, the Queen Anne coal-scuttle, the bagatelle board, the hand organ—all gone, and jewels too. Opals and emeralds, they lie about the roots of turnips. What a scraping paring affair it is to be sure! The wonder is that I've any clothes on my back, that I sit surrounded by solid furniture at this moment. Why, if one wants to compare life to anything, one must liken it to being blown through the Tube at fifty miles an hour—landing at the other end without a single hairpin in one's hair! Shot out at the feet of God entirely naked! Tumbling head over heels in the asphodel meadows like brown paper parcels pitched down a shoot in the post office! With one's hair flying back like the tail of a race-horse. Yes, that seems to express the rapidity of life, the perpetual waste and repair; all so casual, all so haphazard. . . .

But after life. The slow pulling down of thick green stalks so that the cup of the flower, as it turns over, deluges one with purple and red light. Why, after all, should one not be born there as one is born here, helpless, speechless, unable to focus one's eyesight, groping at the roots of the grass, at the toes of the Giants? As for saying which are trees, and which are men and women, or whether there are such things, that one won't be in a condition to do for fifty years or so. There will be nothing but spaces of light and dark, intersected by thick stalks, and rather higher up perhaps, rose-shaped blots of an indistinct colour—dim pinks and blues—which will, as time goes on, become more definite, become—I don't know what. . . .

And yet that mark on the wall is not a hole at all. It may even be caused by some round black substance, such as a small rose leaf, left over from the summer, and I, not being a very vigilant housekeeper—look at the dust on the mantelpiece, for example, the dust which, so they say, buried Troy three times over, only fragments of pots utterly refusing annihilation, as one can believe.

The tree outside the window taps very gently on the pane. . . . I want to think quietly, calmly, spaciously, never to be interrupted, never to have to rise from my chair, to slip easily from one thing to another, without any sense of hostility, or obstacle. I want to sink deeper and deeper, away from the surface, with its hard separate facts. To steady myself, let me catch hold of the first idea that passes. . . . Shakespeare . . . Well, he will do as well as another. A man who sat himself solidly in an arm-chair, and looked into the fire, so—A shower of ideas fell perpetually from some very high Heaven down through his mind. He leant his forehead on his hand, and people, looking in through the open door,—for this scene is supposed to take place on a summer's evening,—But how dull this is, this historical fiction! It doesn't interest me at all. I wish I could hit upon a pleasant track of thought, a track indirectly reflecting credit upon myself, for those are the pleasantest thoughts, and very frequent even in the minds of modest mouse-coloured people, who believe genuinely that they dislike to hear their own praises. They are not thoughts directly praising oneself; that is the beauty of them; they are thoughts like this:

"And then I came into the room. They were discussing botany. I said how I'd seen a flower growing on a dust heap on the site of an old house in Kingsway. The seed, I said, must have been sown in the reign of Charles the First. What flowers grew in the reign of

Charles the First?" I asked—(but I don't remember the answer). Tall flowers with purple tassels to them perhaps. And so it goes on. All the time I'm dressing up the figure of myself in my own mind, lovingly, stealthily, not openly adoring it, for if I did that, I should catch myself out, and stretch my hand at once for a book in self-protection. Indeed, it is curious how instinctively one protects the image of oneself from idolatry or any other handling that could make it ridiculous, or too unlike the original to be believed in any longer. Or is it not so very curious after all? It is a matter of great importance. Suppose the looking glass smashes, the image disappears, and the romantic figure with the green of forest depths all about it is there no longer, but only that shell of a person which is seen by other people—what an airless, shallow, bald, prominent world it becomes! A world not to be lived in. As we face each other in omnibuses and underground railways we are looking into the mirror; that accounts for the vagueness, the gleam of glassiness, in our eyes. And the novelists in future will realize more and more the importance of these reflections, for of course there is not one reflection but an almost infinite number; those are the depths they will explore, those the phantoms they will pursue, leaving the description of reality more and more out of their stories, taking a knowledge of it for granted, as the Greeks did and Shakespeare perhaps—but these generalizations are very worthless. The military sound of the word is enough. It recalls leading articles, cabinet ministers—a whole class of things indeed which as a child one thought the thing itself, the standard thing, the real thing, from which one could not depart save at the risk of nameless damnation. Generalizations bring back somehow Sunday in London, Sunday afternoon walks, Sunday luncheons, and also ways of speaking of the dead, clothes, and habits—like the habit of sitting all together in one room until a certain hour, although nobody liked it. There was a rule for everything. The rule for tablecloths at that particular period was that they should be made of tapestry with little yellow compartments marked upon them, such as you may see in photographs of the carpets in the corridors of the royal palaces. Tablecloths of a different kind were not real tablecloths. How shocking, and yet how wonderful it was to discover that these real things, Sunday luncheons, Sunday walks, country houses, and tablecloths were not entirely real, were indeed half phantoms, and the damnation which visited the disbeliever in them was only a sense of illegitimate freedom. What now takes the place of those things I wonder, those real standard things? Men perhaps, should you be a woman; the masculine point of view which governs our lives, which sets the standard, which establishes Whitaker's Table of Precedency, which has become, I suppose, since the war half a phantom to many men and women, which soon, one may hope, will be laughed into the dustbin where the phantoms go, the mahogany sideboards and the Landseer prints, Gods and Devils, Hell and so forth, leaving us all with an intoxicating sense of illegitimate freedom—if freedom exists. . . .

In certain lights that mark on the wall seems actually to project from the wall. Nor is it entirely circular.

I cannot be sure, but it seems to cast a perceptible shadow, suggesting that if I ran my finger down that strip of the wall it would, at a certain point, mount and descend a small tumulus, a smooth tumulus like those barrows on the South Downs which are, they say, either tombs or camps. Of the two I should prefer them to be tombs, desiring melancholy like most English people, and finding it natural at the end of a walk to think of the bones stretched beneath the turf. . . . There must be some book about it. Some antiquary must have dug up those bones and given them a name. . . . What sort of a man is an antiquary, I wonder? Retired Colonels for the most part, I daresay, leading parties of aged labourers to the top here, examining clods of earth and stone, and getting into correspondence with the neighbouring clergy, which, being opened at breakfast time, gives them a feeling of importance, and the comparison of arrow-heads necessitates cross-country journeys to the county towns, an agreeable necessity both to them and to their elderly wives, who wish to make plum jam or to clean out the study, and have every reason for keeping that great question of the camp or the tomb in perpetual suspension, while the Colonel himself feels agreeably philosophic in accumulating evidence on both sides of the question. It is true that he does finally incline to believe in the camp; and, being opposed, indites a pamphlet which he is about to read at the quarterly meeting of the local society when a stroke lays him low, and his last conscious thoughts are not of wife or child, but of the camp and that arrow-head there, which is now in the case at the local museum, together with the foot of a Chinese murderess, a handful of Elizabethan nails, a great many Tudor clay pipes, a piece of Roman pottery, and the wine-glass that Nelson drank out of—proving I really don't know what.

No, no, nothing is proved, nothing is known. And if I were to get up at this very moment and ascertain that the mark on the wall is really—what shall we say?—the head of a gigantic old nail, driven in two hundred years ago, which has now, owing to the patient attrition of many generations of housemaids, revealed its head above the coat of paint, and is taking its first view of modern life in the sight of a white-walled fire-lit room, what should I gain?—Knowledge? Matter for further speculation? I can think sitting still as well as standing up. And what is knowledge? What are our learned men save the descendants of witches and hermits who crouched in caves and in woods brewing herbs, interrogating shrew-mice and writing down the language of the stars? And the less we honour them as our superstitions dwindle and our respect for beauty and health of mind increases. . . . Yes, one could imagine a very pleasant world. A quiet spacious world, with the flowers so red and blue in the open fields. A world without professors or specialists or house-keepers with the profiles of policemen, a world which one could slice with one's thought as a fish slices the water with his fin, grazing the stems of the water-lilies, hanging suspended over nests of white sea eggs. . . . How peaceful it is down here, rooted in the centre of the world and gazing up through the gray waters, with their sudden gleams of light, and their reflections—If it were not for Whitaker's Almanack—if it were not for the Table of Precedency!

I must jump up and see for myself what that mark on the wall really is—a nail, a rose-leaf, a crack in the wood?

Here is Nature once more at her old game of self-preservation. This train of thought, she perceives, is threatening mere waste of energy, even some collision with reality, for who will ever be able to lift a finger against Whitaker's Table of Precedency? The Archbishop of Canterbury is followed by the Lord High Chancellor; the Lord High Chancellor is followed by the Archbishop of York. Everybody follows somebody, such is the philosophy of Whitaker; and the great thing is to know who follows whom. Whitaker knows, and let that, so Nature counsels, comfort you, instead of enraging you; and if you can't be comforted, if you must shatter this hour of peace, think of the mark on the wall.

I understand Nature's game—her prompting to take action as a way of ending any thought that threatens to excite or to pain. Hence, I suppose, comes our slight contempt for men of action—men, we assume, who don't think. Still, there's no harm in putting a full stop to one's disagreeable thoughts by looking at a mark on the wall.

Indeed, now that I have fixed my eyes upon it, I feel that I have grasped a plank in the sea; I feel a satisfying sense of reality which at once turns the two Archbishops and the Lord High Chancellor to the shadows of shades. Here is something definite, something real. Thus, waking from a midnight dream of horror, one hastily turns on the light and lies quiescent, worshipping the chest of drawers, worshipping solidity, worshipping reality, worshipping the impersonal world which is a proof of some existence other than ours. That is what one wants to be sure of. . . . Wood is a pleasant thing to think about. It comes from a tree; and trees grow, and we don't know how they grow. For years and years they grow, without paying any attention to us, in meadows, in forests, and by the side of rivers—all things one likes to think about. The cows swish their tails beneath them on hot afternoons; they paint rivers so green that when a moorhen dives one expects to see its feathers all green when it comes up again. I like to think of the fish balanced against the stream like flags blown out; and of water-beetles slowly raising domes of mud upon the bed of the river. I like to think of the tree itself: first the close dry sensation of being wood; then the grinding of the storm; then the slow, delicious ooze of sap. I like to think of it, too, on winter's nights standing in the empty field with all leaves close-furled, nothing tender exposed to the iron bullets of the moon, a naked mast upon an earth that goes tumbling, tumbling, all night long. The song of birds must sound very loud and strange in June; and how cold the feet of insects must feel upon it, as they make laborious progresses up the creases of the bark, or sun themselves upon the thin green awning of the leaves, and look straight in front of them with diamond-cut red eyes. . . . One by one the fibres snap beneath the immense cold pressure of the earth, then the last storm comes and, falling, the highest branches drive deep into the ground again. Even so, life isn't done with; there are a million patient, watchful lives still for a tree, all over the world, in bedrooms, in ships, on the pavement, lining rooms where men and women sit after tea, smoking cigarettes. It is full of peaceful thoughts, happy thoughts, this tree. I should like to take each one separately—but something is getting in the way. . . . Where was I? What has it all been about? A tree? A river? The Downs? Whitaker's Almanack? The fields of asphodel? I can't remember a thing. Everything's moving, falling, slipping, vanishing. . . . There is a vast upheaval of matter. Someone is standing over me and saying—

"I'm going out to buy a newspaper."

"Yes?"

"Though it's no good buying newspapers. . . . Nothing ever happens. Curse this war! God damn this war! . . . All the same, I don't see why we should have a snail on our wall."

Ah, the mark on the wall! It was a snail.

M

MACMILLAN COLLECTOR'S LIBRARY

All the books in this series:

A Carnival Jangle by Alice Dunbar Nelson

A Little Cloud by James Joyce

An Unwritten Novel by Virginia Woolf

The Home-Coming by Rabindranath Tagore

Jack and Alice by Jane Austen

The Curious Case of Benjamin Button
by F. Scott Fitzgerald

The Daughters of the Late Colonel
by Katherine Mansfield

The Murders in the Rue Morgue
by Edgar Allan Poe

The Nightingale and the Rose by Oscar Wilde

The Speckled Band by Arthur Conan Doyle